This edition first published
2011 by Brown Watson
The Old Mill, 76 Fleckney Road,
Kibworth Beauchamp, Leic LE8 0HG

ISBN: 978-0-7097-1951-9
© 2011 Brown Watson, England
Reprinted 2011, 2012 (twice)
Printed in Malaysia

Illustrations: Javier Inaraja
Graphic design: Marcela Grez

© TODOLIBRO EDICIONES, S.A.
C/ Campezo, 13 - 28022 Madrid
Tel.: 91 3009115 - Fax: 91 3009110
www.todolibro.es

Classic Fairy Stories

Brown Watson

ENGLAND

Contents

Bambi

All the animals of the forest came together to celebrate the birth of Bambi, the little fawn, son of the Great Prince of the Forest. It was the beginning of a springtime full of adventures.

As soon as Bambi learned to walk, Thumper, the rabbit, took him to meet all the animals of the forest. 'Look, Bambi, a bird!' Thumper would say. 'Bird!' Bambi would repeat.

Winter arrived and the forest was covered in snow. Bambi struggled to keep his balance on the ice. The animals had fun throwing snowballs at each other.

Faline, a doe the same age as Bambi, used to play with them too.

But one day, hunters appeared in the forest, cruelly firing their guns. The terrified animals fled in all directions.
'Run away, my son, don't stop!' Bambi's mother told him. But the hunters fired, and she fell, gravely wounded.

All the animals mourned her loss and tried to console little Bambi. His father, the Great Prince of the Forest, came to him and said:
'The men killed your mother. From now on, I will protect you.'

When spring arrived, Bambi had grown a great deal:he had fine antlers and had been taught all about the forest by his father.

One day he met a beautiful doe:'Hello, Bambi! Don't you recognise me anymore?' It was Faline, who, like him, had grown up and had become a beautiful young creature.

One day, the animals were playing in the forest when, suddenly, a fire began on the horizon.

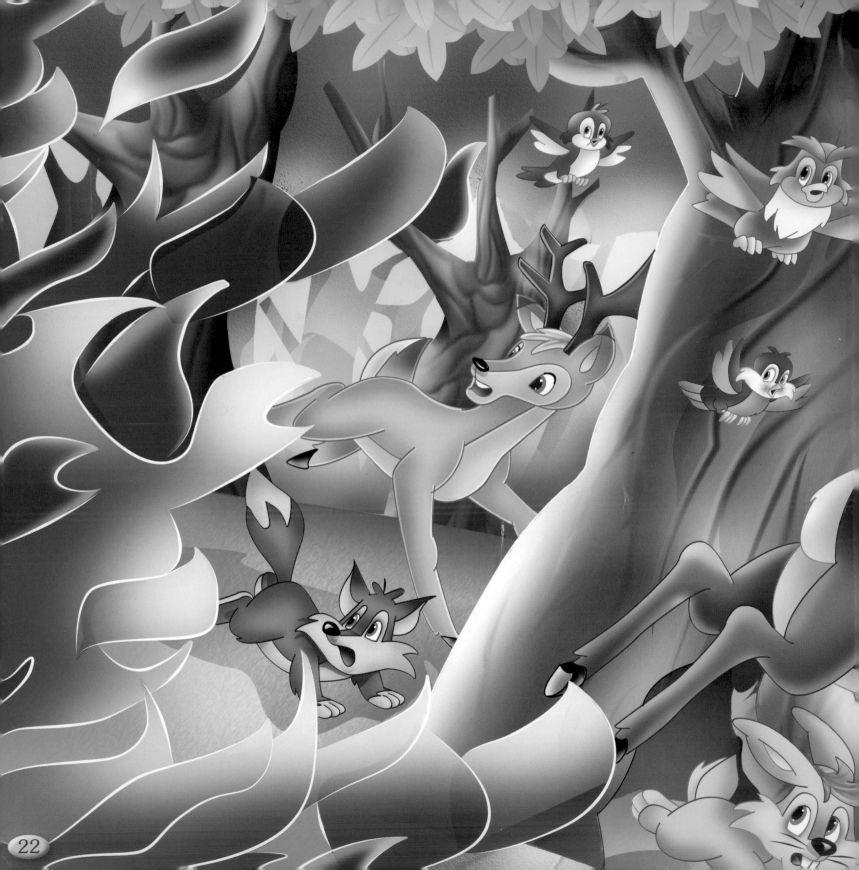

Bambi ran through the forest, warning the animals: 'Everyone go to the island in the river!' he shouted. Together with his father, he saved many animals who could not have crossed the water by themselves.

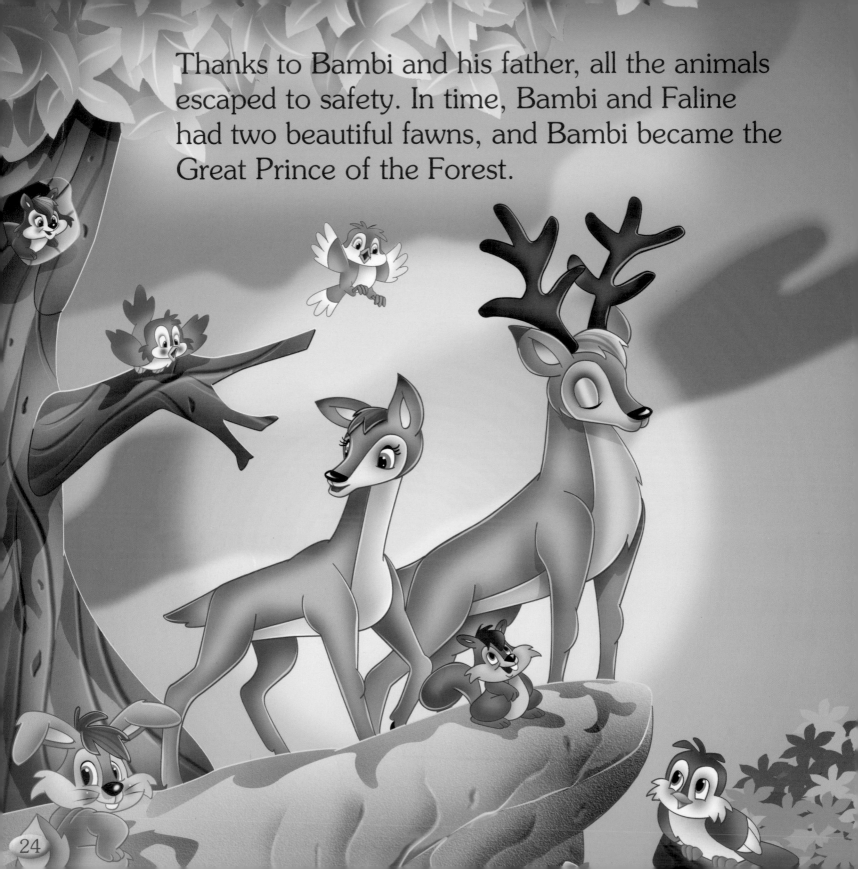

Thanks to Bambi and his father, all the animals escaped to safety. In time, Bambi and Faline had two beautiful fawns, and Bambi became the Great Prince of the Forest.

The Wolf and the Seven Little Goats

Mother Goat lived in the little house in the forest with her seven children. One day she had to go to the market, and she warned her little ones:

'Beware of the wolf and don't open the door; if you open it, he'll eat you.'

Soon afterwards, the wolf knocked at the door of the little goats' house, sweetening his voice: 'Open the door for me, children, it's Mother!'

But the little goats saw the wolf's dark coat. 'No, you're not our mother! Go away, you bad wolf!' the bravest little goat replied.

The cunning wolf waited for the miller to pass by, and covered his paws in flour. He went and knocked again at the door, and showed them one paw. He tricked the little goats, and they opened the door, thinking he was their mother.

31

The wolf leaped on them and ate them up one by one without chewing, so as to eat them as quickly as possible.

33

Only the smallest escaped, by hiding in the old grandfather clock. That was where his mother found him when she came home, happy to see her again.

Mother Goat took her scissors, a needle and thread, and she and her little one went in search of the wolf. With his belly full, he had laid down on the riverbank for a snooze.

Mother Goat cut open the wolf's stomach with her scissors, and the little goats came out safe and happy. Then they filled his stomach with stones, and Mother Goat sewed it shut again.

'How thirsty I am!' roared the wolf when he woke up, and he approached the riverbank to take a drink. But the stones that filled his stomach were so heavy that he fell into the river and drowned.

And from that day on, Mother Goat and her little goats had a peaceful and happy life, with no wolf to trouble them.

The Ugly Duckling

When the mother duck took her children swimming, all the farmyard animals would look at him and laugh:'Good heavens! Poor duck, to be so ugly!' His brothers and sisters were ashamed of him: 'Go away! It's your fault that everyone is staring at us!'

The poor duckling moved so far away from them that he ended up on the opposite bank. Then some shots rang out, and the ugly duckling saw a flock of geese taking flight. The hunters' dogs pursued him furiously.

He managed to escape them, but since he had nowhere to go, he kept on walking. Then winter came…. The animals of the forest watched him with pity, seeing how cold he was.

It snowed and snowed. The ugly duckling hid in an old tree trunk, and there he was found by an old woman and her dog. 'Poor little thing! How ugly and thin he is!' The woman took him home with her.

Here he was taken care of, and he was very happy.
Everyone liked him… everyone except
the jealous cat. 'Since that duck
arrived, nobody pays me any
attention,' he thought.

Spring arrived and the ugly duckling had grown so big that the old woman decided to set him free. The old woman's dog and the jealous cat chased the ugly duckling away from the farm.

He arrived at a pond, where there were two beautiful swans. The duckling thought that they would peck at him. Frightened, he was going to hide his head under his wing when he suddenly saw a beautiful swan reflected in the water – it was none other than himself!

The swans took flight, and the ugly duckling flew with them. As they passed over his old farm, the animals looked up at the sky and exclaimed:
'What beautiful swans!'

The Three Little Pigs

$\mathcal{I}$n a little house in the forest, three little pigs lived happily with their parents. Since they were now fully grown, they decided that each would build his own house.

The first little pig, the laziest in the family, decided to build himself a house of straw. In a moment his house was built, and he sat back to rest.

The second little pig, who was very greedy, preferred to build a house of wood, and began to build it with great enthusiasm.

It didn't take him long and
then he sat down to eat some
apples.

67

The third little pig, who was the hardest worker, built a house of bricks and mortar. It took him a long time to build it, but he made a safe and very handsome house.

Not long afterwards, a hungry wolf approached the first little pig's cabin: 'Open the door, or I'll huff, and I'll puff, and I'll blow your house down!'

The little pig did not open the door, so the wolf huffed and puffed, and the house of straw blew away. The frightened little pig ran to hide in his brother's house.

The wolf followed him and knocked at this door, too:
'Open the door, or I'll blow your house down!'

This little pig would not open the door either, so the wolf huffed and puffed, and the hut fell apart. Terrified, the two little pigs ran to their brother's house.

The wolf knocked at this door, too, and shouted: 'Open the door, or I'll huff, and I'll puff and I'll blow your house down!'

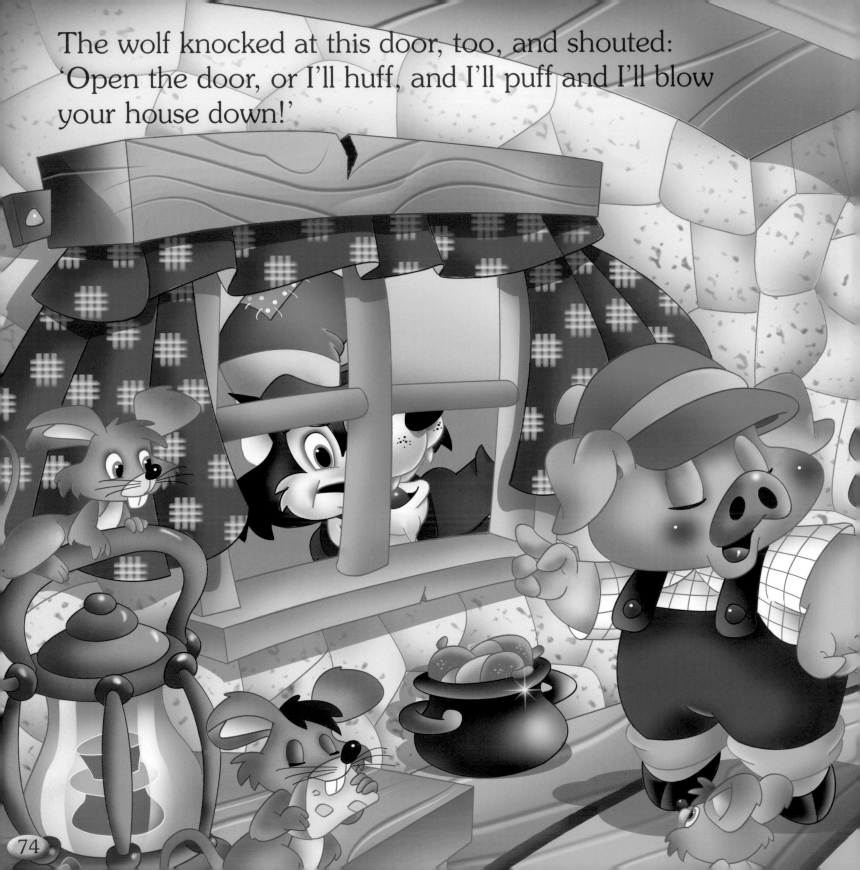

'Blow all you want, but I won't open the door!' said the little pig. The wolf huffed and puffed with all his might, but the house didn't move.

The wolf climbed onto the roof and slid down the chimney. The little pigs put a cauldron of water on to boil, and the wolf fell in. With his tail scalded, he ran away and never came back, and the little pigs lived in peace.

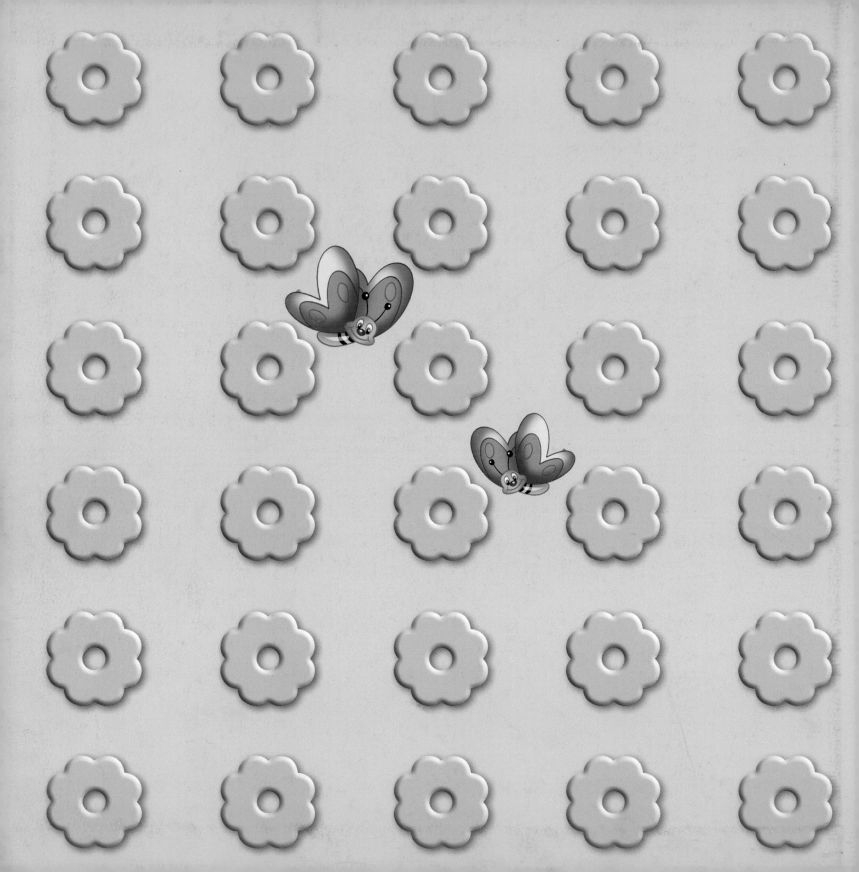